The
Tallest
Tree

The Tallest Tree

Sandra
Belton

Amistad
GREENWILLOW BOOKS
An Imprint of HarperCollins*Publishers*

The Tallest Tree
Copyright © 2008 by Sandra Belton
Amistad is an imprint of HarperCollins Publishers, Inc.
All rights reserved. No part of this book may be used or reproduced in any manner whatsoever without written permission except in the case of brief quotations embodied in critical articles and reviews. Printed in the United States of America. For information address HarperCollins Children's Books, a division of HarperCollins Publishers, 1350 Avenue of the Americas, New York, NY 10019.
www.harpercollinschildrens.com

Page 154 constitutes an extension of the copyright page.

The text of this book is set in 11-point Bell.

Library of Congress Cataloging-in-Publication Data
Belton, Sandra.
The tallest tree / by Sandra Belton.
   p. cm.
"Greenwillow Books."
Summary: When a group of young African-American children learn about Paul Robeson from one of the neighborhood "elders" they decide to reclaim the town theater in order to celebrate Robeson's life.
ISBN: 978-0-06-052749-5 (trade bdg.) ISBN: 978-0-06-052750-1 (lib. bdg.)
1. African Americans—Juvenile fiction. 2. Robeson, Paul, 1898–1976—Juvenile fiction. [1. African Americans—Fiction. 2. Robeson, Paul, 1898-1976—Fiction. 3. Heroes—Fiction.]
I. Title. II. Title: Paul Robeson story.
PZ7.B4197Tal 2008 [Fic]—dc22 2007022476

First Edition 10 9 8 7 6 5 4 3 2 1

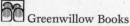 Greenwillow Books

"Those who have no record of what their forebears have accomplished lose the inspiration which comes from the teaching of biography and history."

—CARTER GODWIN WOODSON

As things turned out, it was the only tree left on the street—the one Odell Davis said he stood under when he had his picture taken with Paul Robeson.

"With *who?*" one of the younger boys asked.

"Some dude ain't nobody heard of," one of the older boys answered.

Hearing that, Odell Davis shook his head and looked up at the tree. The only one left.

Of course, it hadn't always been that way. The older folks remembered when trees lined the entire street. On both sides.

"Grand and beautiful, those trees." That's how Pike Howard at the barbershop described the now-gone trees. "Made a body feel proud just standing in their shade."

"Beautiful trees on this street?" the younger boy wondered. Little Catfish, they called him.

The older boy heard this as he watched Hambone Kelly lurching and weaving down the street, filled to the top as usual with too much party making.

"Ain't never been *nothing* beautiful on this street," the boy sneered. Lamar.

The trees weren't the only things that had vanished from the street. The Lakeside Bank had closed. The building was still there, but nothing was inside and most of the windows were boarded up.

All the windows and doors were boarded up in the bread factory. Every kneader, baker, and packager who worked there had been laid off. Like old Maurice.

Nowadays the short bald man who had been in charge of the huge ovens was often found just sitting on the curb, holding a sax nobody but him could see, making music nobody but him could hear. When those ovens were shut down for good, the delicious baking-bread smells old Maurice loved most vanished like his job had.

It was the same up and down the street. The clothes shop had closed. The one called the Quality Shop before Mr. Pickus sold it. Slim's Shoe Salon took over that spot, but it had closed too. So had Waddell's Jewelry, although its gate of black iron diamonds was still locked tight.

Nelson's Cafe on the corner was still open, but not for dinner anymore. Charlie Nelson shut off his deep-fry grill by three o'clock. After that there was only the smell of those crispy, sweet catfish filets he was famous for.

For many, the saddest leaving of all was the dancing mar-quee at the Regal Theater. In its heyday the Regal had been a beautiful city palace. The brilliant square of its marquee was a crown of twinkling lights, skipping around the names of the famous musicians and actors who appeared there.

Roland Hayes.

Marian Anderson.

Lena Horne.

Josephine Baker.

Count Basie.

Ethel Waters.

Duke Ellington.

Paul Robeson.

People had come to the Regal from miles and miles to see these stars. To hear them. But times got tough—lost jobs, small money. The Regal could no longer afford to bring big stars to town. For a while the owners showed movies on the grand stage, announcing the titles on the marquee where the names of stars had been. But then the crown of lights skipped into darkness, and all the music that had filled the street with promise became silence.

These days the Regal was a community center. There were yoga classes most Mondays and tai chi classes on Thursdays. Lamar kept waiting for a karate class to get started. His fourteen-year-old self decided karate was the only ancient art he needed to bother about knowing.

Little Catfish came to the center every Wednesday after school and on Saturday mornings for chess classes. He was quite good at the game, especially having started only a year ago when he was seven.

There were classes for adults, too. Little Catfish's grandmother signed up for a pottery class every time one was offered. Said it kept her fingers nimble.

Once in a while the New Bethel A.M.E. Church would have something in what had been the Regal's main auditorium. Events to raise money, like recitals and concerts. But lately these events happened less and less.

"Humph! This neighborhood has changed too much for them fancy church ladies," Sugar Johnson said. "Like that Mrs. Taylor-Jones woman. You know the one I'm talking about. Used to drive a big green car. Her husband's law office was down the street."

Sugar Johnson had lived on that street for many years and knew it well. She spent long, alone hours on her front stoop. "Yeah, everything's changed 'round here," she would say, looking left and right while her eyes shifted into narrow. Especially when she saw Lamar and his pals strolling past on their way to nowhere in particular.

"And it sure ain't changed for the better. Humph!"

For Little Catfish, the neighborhood hadn't changed much at all. It was pretty much the way it had been for as long as he had lived there—which was all his life. He had never seen anybody pass through the bread factory doors to go to work. He had never gone to Nelson's for dinner. Just for lunch. As far as he knew, his mama had never

Sandra Belton

shopped at Slim's or Waddell's. Or any other place in the neighborhood. She even took two buses to get to the store where she liked to buy groceries.

"Prices at that corner store are too high," she said to Little Catfish when he grumbled about the long ride they had to take to the supermarket. "Plus, the fruits and vegetables they have aren't all that fresh."

But there were times Little Catfish knew in the deep part of him that something *was* missing. Like just before dark when the streets seemed too still. Not filled with noises like the ones in those family stories on TV. And right after bedtime when it was never quite quiet enough.

Little Catfish tried not to think about what might be missing. Instead, he decided that everything he needed was there: his mama and grandma and their small apartment above Mr. Pike Howard's barbershop.

And, of course, there was Mr. Odell.

Odell Davis—Mr. Odell, most everybody called him— had been living in the neighborhood for as long as anybody could remember.

"Odell's been around here even longer than me," Sugar Johnson said, shaking her head. "Humph! That man is old as dirt."

Nobody was sure how old Mr. Odell was. Over time, the only changing thing to notice was his hair. In the early days, it had been like a black cap hugging his head. In the nineteen seventies, that cap grew into a thick, proud halo. As more years passed, the halo turned silver and stretched into locks.

In every way that mattered, Odell Davis didn't change at all. He still spoke with a deep voice that seemed to be resting on the edge of a song. He still towered over most people and had a tendency to look down and sideways while he listened to whatever it was they had to say. His laugh still bubbled up from inside before it burst out loud and full.

Most of all, Odell Davis remained solid. Someone who could always be counted on. Just like that old tree.

And so he was on that early-summer day when Little Catfish headed in the direction of the Regal. Walking in a definitely-going-someplace way, he was counting on Mr. Odell to be there. Or somewhere very close by. Like everybody else, Little Catfish knew Mr. Odell always turned his keys in the locks of the Regal's brass double doors by eight o'clock in the morning. Except on Sundays when he got there around one thirty, shortly after church.

And except on that same day when he closed up around six, Odell Davis was inside or outside the old theater-now-center until shortly after ten at night.

Sure enough, Mr. Odell was sitting just outside the Regal door. "Hey, little man," he called, seeing Little Catfish. "Where you rushing to?"

Little Catfish slowed down. "Nowhere but here." His breath was full of relief. He gave Mr. Odell a wide grin.

Coming up behind Little Catfish was Lamar and one of his hanging-around buddies. Cheeks, Lamar called him. The two boys had been trailing Little Catfish for several blocks. Daring, teasing in their usual way. Now, catching up and seeing Mr. Odell, they slouched on, cutting their eyes at the two by the door and barely saying, "Hey."

"What you up to, boys," Mr. Odell said as they passed.

"How come you always trying to get in my business, old man?" Lamar mumbled behind him. Feeling like punching something, but thinking smarter. And needing to say something to show off for his friend.

"Sure wish you had business I wanted to get into, Lamar," Mr. Odell called to the two slumped-over backs making their way down the sidewalk. "Sure do wish that," he said again, more to himself this time.

Little Catfish settled himself in the other folding chair Mr. Odell always set out next to his own. Now he could relax. Besides, a chance to sit with Mr. Odell was better than most things he could think about doing. Even if all they did was say nothing while they watched the early summer winds blow on that old tree. The only one left.

"Mr. Odell," Little Catfish asked, wiggling a little to see how the afternoon sun painted his shadow. "Did you really have your picture taken under the tree with that man?"

"What man is that?" Mr. Odell leaned back in his narrow metal chair, resting it against the Regal's brick wall.

"You know. That man you said. That Paul Robeson man."

"How come you ask like that, Little Catfish?" Mr. Odell watched his young friend lean his chair back the same way.

"Because that man, he was famous. How you know somebody famous?"

"And how do *you* know he was famous?" Mr. Odell looked sideways at Little Catfish.

"'Cause I saw a book about him at the library and remembered what you said. You know, about being with him in a picture." It was easy to hear that Little Catfish was pleased with himself. "I checked that book out. It has a bunch of pages. With all those pages, he *must* be famous. For something."

"Yep, he was famous, all right." Mr. Odell stretched out his long legs and crossed one ankle over the other. "And for a whole bunch of somethings."

"Like what?"

"Like just about any something you want to mention."
Mr. Odell's laugh started to bubble.

And so it happened just that way. Without anybody
realizing it at the time, something new on that street got
planted.

Little Catfish

Sometimes I wish Mr. Odell was my daddy. He's probably too old, but that's okay. Maybe he could be my granddaddy.

My grandma, Nana Rose, says I had a good granddaddy and that I look like him. His name was Winston. I never even met him. Nana Rose keeps his picture on the table by the couch. The one I sleep on. I see that picture every night before I turn off the light and think I don't look like Mr. Granddaddy Winston at all.

Mama says I look like my father. He lived here when I was little, but I don't remember him. He went away to fight in a war and never came back. The only picture I've seen of my dad is one when he was a kid. In that picture he doesn't look anything like me, but maybe he started looking that way when he grew up. Maybe that's why Mama says I look like him.

I don't look like Mr. Odell at all. But that's okay. He could still be in my family.

I bet Mama and Nana Rose would like Mr. Odell just as much as I do if they had a chance to. Like hearing him talk like he does. He knows about a whole lot of stuff. And I bet he knows everything there is to know about Mr. Paul Robeson.

At first I could hardly believe some of the stuff Mr. O. was telling me. Like about Mr. Paul Robeson being a great football player AND a great basketball player AND a great baseball player. But now I know what he said was true. Every bit of it. All of it was in the book I got from the library.

I asked Nana Rose to help me read some of the things in that book. Then one day when I was looking for the book and couldn't find it, she told me where to look. She had slipped it under her bed. She said she heard about Mr. Paul Robeson when she was *growing up and would like to read more about him herself.*

Maybe one day Mama and Nana Rose will let me invite Mr. Odell over to dinner. Then all of us can talk about Mr. Did-Practically-Everything Paul Robeson.

Summer came and just sat down. The days got hot, then hotter. Burning-up days that smiled at people living on the edges of the city—places with tall, grand trees spreading shade in all directions. But those same days laughed out loud at people living in the middle of the city. Like the ones on the street with just one tree left.

That summer heat became one of the counted-on things. Like Mr. Odell and Little Catfish being together. Almost every day while the temperature climbed, there the two of them would be. Sitting outside the Regal or just inside the folds of the wide brass doors. Or walking slow from somewhere like the flavored-ice stand set up where the hardware store used to be. Or maybe just standing under that tree.

But sitting, standing, or strolling along, they were together. Usually deep in talk. Sometimes laughing, sometimes looking serious, and a few other times difficult to tell which.

"Hard to figure what them two is up to," Sugar Johnson would mutter whenever she saw them. "Hard to figure at all. Humph!"

For Little Catfish, being with Mr. Odell was summer camp and Little League all rolled into one. His mama had promised sleepaway camp soon, but not that year. "Money's too tight right now, baby," she had said. "Next summer for sure."

As for Little League, Pike Howard had tried to get a group started. He kept after the alderman to clean up the vacant lot next to the locked-up jewelry store so the kids could have a safe place to play. But the city elections were over, and the next ones a long way off. Getting an already-elected alderman to follow up on all those "gonna-be" campaign promises was . . . well, not always an easy thing to do.

Except for patches of scraggly grass and smatters of broken glass poking their dangerous edges almost any-where, that lot stayed just like it was. Even worse, Lamar and his running buddies claimed the space as their place for summer and dared anyone—especially the little kids—to come anywhere near it.

"Whatchu want?" Lamar challenged one day as Little Catfish passed by. Walking slow. Looking and wondering what the big boys were into.

"Nothin'," Little Catfish said, looking down at his tennis shoes and moving faster.

"And that's all you know," Lamar called back to him.

"Nothin'! You or that old man you always with. Actin' like he your hero or something. Truth is, neither y'all about nothin' and don't know nothin' either!"

Little Catfish felt Lamar's words against his back as he hurried along. Rushing to reach the Regal just a little farther down the way. Rushing and thinking how right and how wrong Lamar was all at the same time.

"Hey, Mr. Odell," Little Catfish said, settling himself in the companion chair. "Remember when you were first telling me about Mr. Paul Robeson and how awesome he was as an athlete? How he played football, basketball, *and* baseball?"

"*And* track," Mr. Odell said, nodding his head.

"Yeah," Little Catfish said. "And then the other day you were talking about how smart Mr. Paul Robeson was. How he won a scholarship to college and then graduated from college at the top of his class. Remember?"

Mr. Odell kept nodding his head. "At the *very* top of his college class. And then went on to law school. Finished that, too, but he didn't like being a lawyer all that much."

"And yesterday, Mr. O.?" Little Catfish looked into his friend's eyes. "Remember how you told me how good Mr. Paul Robeson sang? How he was even famous as a singer?"

Mr. Odell kept nodding. He added a chuckle. "Yes indeed, he had a magnificent voice. Traveled all over the world giving concerts."

Little Catfish moved closer. "Know what, Mr. O.?" he said. "Last night me and Nana Rose was reading in my book and found something about Mr. Paul Robeson being an actor. How he acted somewhere in New York City called Broadway. And how he even acted in movies!"

As the young boy moved closer and looked into Mr. Odell's eyes, his own eyes grew narrow. Perhaps his way of looking deeper. Hoping to see for certain what those old eyes would show when they heard what he had to say next.

"Mr. Odell, can't *nobody* be all that! It just ain't possible!"

Little Catfish's words tumbled out, getting louder as they fell.

The dark brown eyes staring back at Little Catfish didn't so much as flicker. The truth in them was as easy to see as the head they were in, and that was moving up and down.

"Hard to believe, but it's all true," Mr. Odell said. "Every bit of it. And more!"

"*More?*" Little Catfish's voice and eyelids rose with surprise.

Mr. Odell laughed. "*Lots* more," he said. "And in my opinion, some of that 'more' is the best part about Paul Robeson."

"What's better than being smarter than just about

anybody? *Plus*, being able to play practically every kind of sport invented!" Little Catfish shook his head from side to side. "Uhn-un, Mr. O. No way. Can't nothing can be better than that!"

Mr. Odell sat back in his chair. "Got to disagree with you there, little man," he said. "In my opinion one of the greatest things about Paul Robeson was how he went to bat for *right!*"

"Huh?" Little Catfish's eyes were wide as he turned to look again at Mr. Odell. "I don't understand."

As Mr. Odell leaned closer to explain, his silver locks moved across his shoulders. "It's like this, little man," he said. "Paul Robeson was a fighter in the best sense of the word. He put himself on the line for and fought for the things he believed in."

"Like what?" Little Catfish moved closer.

With their heads close together, the two once again got deep into talk. Neither seemed even to notice the tall slim boy passing in front of them. Lamar. Alone for once. Slouching his way down the street with one of his hands bunched into the pocket of his jeans and the other holding a can of spray paint.

Lamar

One of these days I'm going to tag that old piece of building. Yeah. When I finish, old man Odell won't even be able to find the door. Yeah. He'll come walking all fast down the street like he does every morning. Rushing to that raggedy old piece of has-been. Only when he gets there, he won't know it. Yeah.

Maybe I'll do a picture of Bruce Lee. And Jet Li. Yeah. Maybe even Billy Jack. They some bad dudes. Talk about knowing how to fight—I bet they can whip anybody!

Yeah. That's what I'll do. Tag that center with pictures of some real heroes. None of those old-timey dudes old man Odell keeps dreaming up. Soon as I get me some new tips, that's exactly what I'm going to do. Can't do nothing with the tips on the cans now. My markers are shot too.

Maybe I should ask Aunt Lou for some money. Nah. She'd just say what she always says. How she has to make sure the other kids have stuff they need. How there's no money left over by the end of the month.

Aunt Lou says maybe I should ask my moms for some money. That my moms is always saying how much she cares about me. But saying ain't doing. If she cares so much, how come I'm not with her? How come she's hardly ever around? Yeah. If I had to depend on her for anything, I'd be clear out of luck.

Maybe I should say something to Cheeks. He said that wall I tagged in the lot was the bomb. Yeah. Maybe Cheeks can lend me a few coins for some tips.

If that raggedy center was worth anything, it'd have some decent supplies for people to use. And decent karate classes. But that place is good for nothing. And except for conning little kids, neither is old man Odell. Yeah. Nothing!

That summer turned out to be one of the hottest on record. Maybe that's why it burned itself out early. Folks started feeling the coming-winds of fall even before the end of August.

One especially cool day Mr. Odell and Little Catfish moved their conversation into Pike Howard's barbershop. It was always a friendly place and usually lively. Like today, with Billy Bradshaw hanging around, waiting his turn to be in Pike's chair.

Billy B., as the young man was best known, had grown up on the street during better times. He could remember the chatter and laughter of folks on their way to work and the delicious smells of baking bread. When he finished high school, he was awarded a scholarship to attend college in another part of the country. "One of them big, fancy schools," Sugar Johnson had said. "Humph. That's the last we'll see of that boy!"

But Sugar Johnson was wrong. After he graduated from that school *and* one more besides, Billy came back. He didn't live on the street anymore but visited the neighborhood on a regular basis. His Auntie Evelyn still lived there. And Pike Howard was still his only barber.

Billy B. was a favorite of most everybody. Especially the kids. He always took time for them and made it special. Like he did that day.

"What you up to, little man?" Billy said to Little Catfish, throwing friendly punches into the air around the young boy. Air boxing.

"Nothing much," Little Catfish said, bobbing and

dodging between the pretend punches.

"Soon you'll be up to plenty," Billy B. said, beginning to dance around, egging Little Catfish to do the same. "School'll be starting in a couple of weeks."

"Yeah, I know," Little Catfish said, trying to get a foot rhythm going with the trim young man.

Billy B. reached over to put Little Catfish's right arm in a better position, then hopped back to encourage him to use it. "I know you'll be ready for school, Little Cat. You been having your nose in one kind of book or another all summer."

Little Catfish's next punch was right on the mark. "Yeah," he said, grinning. Proud of himself even though his target was only the air.

"There you go, buddy! Good one!" Billy B. patted Little Catfish on the back.

"Mr. B.," Little Catfish said, still dancing around while he looked into Billy Bradshaw's face. "You know about

Mr. Paul Robeson who did all kinds of stuff? Did you know he was a fighter too?"

A smile slid across Billy B.'s face. But before he could get his next words out, Lamar stepped into the shop. He had been passing by and noticed the sparring going on inside. Stopping, he had overheard a word here and there.

Lamar moved farther in. "You saying that Robinson guy was a big-time fighter?" he said, tucking his thumbs into the loops of his jeans.

"Robeson," Little Catfish mumbled, but not loud enough for Lamar to hear.

"The name is ROBE-son, young man," Mr. Odell repeated in a voice loud enough for the entire shop to hear. "Robeson. Paul Leroy Robeson."

Lamar shrugged his shoulders. "Whatever," he said, narrowing his eyes at Mr. Odell. Then looking again at Billy, he kept on. "Anyway, if the man was such a hotshot fighter, he probably knew karate." Lamar threw back his shoulders. "Yeah, he probably knew karate. That's the kind of fighting I'm gonna learn how to do. Yeah. Karate."

Mr. Odell leaned forward in the barber chair he was sitting in. The one Pike Howard's nephew used for his customers on the days he worked there. Mr. Odell was about to speak, but Billy Bradshaw held up his hand. A signal. *He* wanted this chance to straighten out Lamar.

"Wait up," Billy Bradshaw said. He moved closer to Lamar. To look directly in his face and speak into his eyes. "First of all, that's not the kind of fighting we were talking about. But even if it were, you got the wrong idea about karate, my man. That's one of them ancient arts. One where you defend yourself with your bare hands. Fact is, that's what the word means: 'empty hands.'"

Billy Bradshaw took one more step closer to Lamar. "When folks decide to use ka-ra-te," he said, pushing out the word with three strong beats, "they do so without any purpose of harm or evil. They do it *only* to defend themselves. *Only* that."

Billy B. stretched out his fingers, suddenly realizing that his hands had still been balled into fists. "Fact is, Paul Robeson was one of the greatest black fighters ever. But he fought with his mind. With his *words!*"

"How?" Lamar's question slipped out even though he hadn't meant for it to.

This time Mr. Odell didn't stop himself from jumping back into the conversation. "Like speaking out about *wrong* wherever he saw it. Anywhere in the world!"

Pike Howard decided to take his turn. Still holding the clippers he was using, he stepped in front of the customer in his barber chair. "That's right," Pike said. "Anywhere and anybody! Paul Robeson saw how soldiers were being segregated in the American armed forces and spoke out against it. He marched in support of laborers in England. He performed concerts in Spain to raise money for the troops."

The customer decided to jump in as well. "And money wouldn't make him go against what he believed either," the man said. Mr. Coltrane. A regular who came for a hair and beard trim every two weeks. "That man refused to give concerts to any audience that was segregated," Mr. Coltrane said. "Where black people couldn't attend or had to sit in a special place. He wouldn't do it no matter how much money they were going to pay him."

Watching and listening, Little Catfish couldn't keep himself from joining the chorus of men. "Yeah," he said, "and Mr. Paul Robeson went on marches to protest stuff just like Dr. King did. Only way before Dr. King did. And Mr. Paul Robeson could speak a bunch of languages, so he went on protests in places all over . . ." Seeing the mean look on Lamar's face, Little Catfish's voice grew softer and softer until it had faded away.

Billy Bradshaw gently smoothed his hand across Little Catfish's head and took over. "Right you are, Little Cat," he said. "But, you want to know something else, Lamar? If Paul Robeson *had* taken up karate, I bet he would have been one heck of a champ. A real karate hero! In *true* karate-do, the fighter is completely devoted to justice. Yes indeed, completely!"

Mr. Odell, Mr. Coltrane, and Pike Howard all nodded their heads along with an "Un-huh" amen chorus. "And that's what Paul Robeson was," Mr. Odell added. "A true-life hero!"

All the faces in the shop were smiling. Except Lamar's. From his scowl came the sound of sucking teeth and a mumbled, "He ain't no hero of mine!" Then he turned and headed out the door, muttering "Forget you!" Or something like that.

Little Catfish watched the back of the older boy grow smaller as Lamar made his way down the street. Then, without completely understanding what led him to think it, Little Catfish said out loud what was on his mind. "You know something? I think Lamar needs a hero."

Mr. Odell had held himself from going after the young blood now storming his way down the street. From calling out his name and trying to command him to just listen. Now as he looked down at his young friend, a smile began to warm in his eyes. "You know something, little man," he said, "you might have something there. Yep, you just might."

And so it happened that just like that, the new thing that had gotten planted on that street began to take root.

Little Catfish

I hate wintertime! Nana Rose says it's not good to hate any-
thing, but I can't help it. Wintertime stinks. Especially after
Christmas when there's nothing to look forward to.

I sure do miss Mr. Odell. I haven't seen him for weeks and
weeks and weeks! Mama says it hasn't been all that long, but it
has. She said remember how we saw him the other day when we
were on the way home from the grocery store. Mr. O. was walk-
ing down the street. I said that didn't count. We were on the
bus, and I couldn't even say hello. Mama said it counted because
I saw him. It didn't, though.

I didn't even see him when I went to the center for my chess
lesson. I didn't see anybody. The only thing there to see was a

big sign saying the center was closed because the furnace was broken and there wasn't any heat.

I hope somebody fixes that furnace. Mama said the heat went off in the little food shop down the street and never came back on. They locked up that shop for good.

I just got to see Mr. Odell soon. I want to show him the memory book I been working on at school. Teacher said everybody had to make one about somebody we want other people to know about. My friend Roman is doing his about his grandfather, who he used to live with in Cuba. He misses him a lot. Nana Rose said I should do mine about my grandfather. But I don't miss Mr. Granddaddy Winston because I never even met him.

I never even met Mr. Paul Robeson either. But it feels like I know him. And I miss him because I'm not around Mr. Odell to talk about him like we do.

I sure hope Mr. O. is okay.

Winter that year was especially long. Unfriendly. Pale skies, bitter cold. Most days the streets looked the same as the tree. Close to dead. Nothing much going on that anyone could see.

Rumors were going around about the broken-down furnace at the Regal. How it couldn't be fixed. That a new one was going to have to be installed. Nobody seemed to know for sure the truth about the matter. But whatever it was, the Regal stayed closed all through March.

"Humph! I knew that center wouldn't last," Sugar Johnson said to Little Catfish's mother at the bus stop one day. "That's the end of that place. *Nothing* even halfway good lasts around here. Humph!"

* * *

Finally, *finally*, the sweet winds of April blew in. Bit by bit, friendly whispering breezes drifted in and seemed ready to settle down. Spring at last.

Early in the morning of that first we're-hoping-spring-for-sure day, street noises coming through the opened living-room window hummed Little Catfish awake. The crispy smell of fresh fish frying tickled at his nose and pushed him out of bed. In only minutes he was brushed, dressed, and ready to run to Nelson's to pick up the catfish filets his mother said he could buy to go with the eggs she was going to cook for breakfast.

Running down the outside steps Little Catfish almost ran into Roman, who rolled up on his skateboard. "Hey, buddy," Little Catfish said, happy to see his friend.

"*Hola*, Douglass!" said Roman. He had the habit of calling Little Catfish by the name their teacher used every day in their classroom. "Want to go boarding? Like at the old ditch?"

"Hey, great!" Little Catfish said, looking down at the board now motionless under Roman's foot. "But I have to check on something first. And I gotta pick up some fish at Nelson's. Oh, and after that I have to eat breakfast. Can you wait? Maybe you can eat something too."

Roman grabbed up his board. "Okay," he said, following behind Little Catfish, who had started moving quickly ahead. "What do you have to check out?"

Jogging in front, Little Catfish spoke over his shoulder. "My friend Mr. Odell. You know. The one I was telling you about."

"How come you have to check him out?" Roman called, almost running to keep up with his friend. "Is he sick or something?"

Hearing this, Little Catfish slowed down. "I just haven't seen him in a long time," he said. The possibility of Mr. Odell *not* being okay was something he tried to keep out of his thoughts.

Roman caught up with Little Catfish, putting the two side by side as the Regal came into view. When they saw what was straight ahead, both of them stopped.

It wasn't the flung-open doors of the Regal that held their attention, although seeing them made Little Catfish smile with relief. And it wasn't the set-out-like-usual fold-up chairs, although this sight changed the smile into a grin. What caught and held both pairs of eyes was the marquee.

Hanging above Mr. Odell's chairs and blowing gently in the wind was a sign on the marquee. Not *in* the marquee with the dancing lights from the good old times, but a drawn-up sign. A wide sheet of paper fastened to the marquee with a long piece of string. Or something like that.

"What's that?" Roman said.

Little Catfish looked at the letters printed on the sign and started putting them together. "'RE-TRO-SPEC-TIVE,'" he read out loud, giving each part of the word its own small song.

"What's that?" Roman asked again, this time meaning the word as much as the sign.

Right then, almost as if he had been waiting for this moment, Mr. Odell walked through the opened doors of the Regal. "Retro-*spec*-tive," he said. He was going to say more, but Little Catfish didn't give him a chance.

"Mr. O.! Where you been? I'm really glad to see you!" Little Catfish's happy words kept rushing out. "Now you can meet my friend. His name's Roman. He's in my room at school. I been telling him about you. And about Mr. Paul Robeson, too."

Mr. Odell grinned at the two boys. "Glad to meet you, Roman," he said, stretching out his hand to shake Roman's.

"Me too, Mr. O——, ah, Mr. . . ." Roman stopped. He didn't quite know how to finish the name.

"Mr. Odell," Little Catfish said, still grinning. "Sometimes *I* call him Mr. O. for short 'cause we're good friends."

Roman nodded his head, understanding. "Ah, Mr. Odell, what's that sign for?"

Mr. Odell looked up at the sign just as the two boys were doing. "It's announcing a retrospective!" he said, giving the word a long, proud sound. "A retrospective is a kind of looking back, you might say."

"Looking back at what?" both boys asked at the same time.

"Come on inside and see for yourself," Mr. Odell invited.

And so they did.

Inside, the old theater seemed pretty much like always. Dim. Musty. The faded red carpet still covered the wide lobby floor from corner to corner. Pieces of gold paint still peeled off the curving banisters on both sides of the stairs leading up to the dark of the mezzanine. The figures painted years and years ago on the rounded ceiling still looked down at everything through a fog of dust.

But there were differences. High and low, here and there. As his eyes adjusted to the dim lights, Little Catfish begin to see them.

First, the posters. Big ones, small ones, some in black and white, some in color. All of them taped to the facing walls on either side of the lobby, showing faces of people and events long past.

* **Cab Calloway:** The Hi De Ho Man
* The Films of **Oscar Micheaux**
* **Countee Cullen** Reads "Yet Do I Marvel"
* Toast Of Paris: **Josephine Baker**
* Renowned Tenor: **Roland Hayes**
* A Conversation with **Booker T. Washington**
* **Duke Ellington** & His Orchestra
* **Bill Pickett:** America's Cowboy
* **Lena Horne** & **Katherine Dunham** In *Stormy Weather*, starring **Ossie Davis**
* **Harry Belafonte:** A Living Legend
* Highlights From *Porgy and Bess*: Featuring **William Warfield**

Little Catfish walked farther in, searching the walls for a face, a name he recognized. Then he saw high above some of the posters a sign printed with letters like the one hanging outside the theater.

THE TREES OF OUR FOREST

Next to the sign, placed higher than anything else, was a picture of Paul Robeson. Under it was a third sign, printed like the other two.

OUR TALLEST TREE

"Wow," said Little Catfish. Then he breathed the word again. "Wow."

Spread out below that sign were pictures and headlines cut out from magazines and newspapers. All of them about Paul Robeson.

Paul Robeson . . . the baseball player, basketball player, and All-American football player . . . the Phi Beta Kappa scholar, head of his class in college . . . graduating from law school, the only black man in his class . . . the singer . . . the actor . . . the movie star . . . the fighter against wrong.

Little Catfish got as close to the wall as he could get, craning his neck as far as it could go. "Mr. O.," he called to his friend who was still standing near the door, "where'd you get all this stuff?"

"Oh, a little here and there and anywhere," Mr. Odell said. His voice made a small echo under the high curved ceiling.

Roman hadn't moved much beyond the box office counter near the door. It had been bare, not used for anything since the Regal closed. Now stacks of books stretched up behind it and out across it. Beside the counter was the beat-up leather sofa Mr. Odell often took naps on, and beside the sofa was an old scratched-up table with an old-fashioned record player on top and a stack of LP record albums underneath.

Roman looked at the piles of books and records. "Hey, Douglass," he called out, hoping his voice would make an echo too. "There's stuff over here, too, about that man in your memory book. There's stuff about a lot of people."

"Mr. O.," Little Catfish said, looking back at Mr. Odell. "Are you making a museum or something? It sure looks like it."

The words just made it out of Little Catfish's mouth when he heard them again. "And it sure looks like *you're* in trouble, little boy," these words said. They came from Little Catfish's mom.

Little Catfish hated his mother calling him "little boy." He also knew he had done or *not* done something whenever she did. Then he remembered. "The fish!" he said.

"Right," his mother said, walking into the theater lobby. "Nana Rose and I been waiting and waiting for you. Just like the eggs and toast were waiting for the rest of our breakfast to get there."

Little Catfish looked down at the worn carpet to avoid looking into his mother's face. "Sorry, Mama," he said. "I'll go right now."

"Too late now," his mother said, walking into the old theater. "The eggs were getting cold, so we went on ahead and ate." She walked farther in, looking around her as she came. "What's all this?"

Mr. Odell moved beside Little Catfish's mother, Grace Walker. "Ms. Grace," he said, using the name he had called her since she was a teenager, "I thought I'd put together a little something to help us remember some of our greatest heroes."

Mrs. Walker walked closer to the wall her son had been staring at. "So that's what the sign out front is all about," she said, leaning in to see the display better. "'The trees of our forest . . .'" she read as she looked.

"Look, Mama!" Little Catfish pointed above him. "There's a bunch of stuff up there about Mr. Paul Robeson."

"I see," his mother said, beginning to examine the wall more closely. "My goodness, Mr. Odell, this is an incredible collection. Where'd you find all this stuff?"

"Mr. O. told us he found a little here and there and anywhere," Little Catfish said, glad to have his mom off his case about the missing fish.

Mr. Odell chuckled. "A lot of these old posters turned up right here," he said. "In this building. I found them during all the moving around in the basement to see what could be done about the furnace. I also had a little collecting help. When Pike found out what I was doing, he threw in some old *Ebony* and *Jet* magazines and *Defender* and *Pittsburgh Courier* newspapers for me to look

through. Said he had been keeping them around for posterity and that a display like this was the best posterity he
could think of."

"Wow," Little Catfish said again. It was the only thing
he could think of to say, and that one word said it all.

Quietly the four made their way through the Regal's
lobby, each with a special purpose. Little Catfish's mom
didn't want to miss anything taped to the walls while her
son hoped to see everything posted about Paul Robeson.
Roman moved from the corner to get his first real look at
the inside of the old theater he had wondered about every
time he had passed it. Mr. Odell kept himself pretty much
in the center of the lobby, ready to answer any questions
he hoped they'd have.

"This is something else, Mr. Odell," Mrs. Walker said.
"Something else!" Her eyes remained on the walls as she
moved slowly along beside them. "I'm going to tell Mama
to come over here. She'll want to see this!"

"Tell *everybody* to do that," Mr. Odell said. "It's everybody's retrospective!"

Still examining each curve and rise of the huge open space, Roman was the first to see another sign. It was taped to the closed heavy doors leading to the main auditorium.

FREE MOVIE INSIDE

"Hey, Mr. Odell," he said, truly excited for the first time that day. "Is this sign right? This one about the movie?"

"It's going to be," Mr. Odell said. "As soon as things get going, there'll be free movies *and* free popcorn."

"Really, Mr. O.?" Little Catfish came over to see the sign for himself. "Will there be any movies showing Mr. Paul Robeson?"

"Yep, those too."

"When, Mr. O.? When?" Little Catfish almost jumped out of his shoes with excitement.

"Not until after you've had some breakfast," his mother answered. "That's the very next thing you're going to be looking at."

For a moment Little Catfish's next words went back and forth in his mind. Then he decided just to let them out. "Mama, can I still go to Nelson's to get some catfish? And can I get some for Roman, too?"

There was only a flash of silence before Mrs. Walker gave her answer. "Sure, son," she said, smiling at the two boys. "Run on to Nelson's and then straight back home."

The two boys said their "See-you-laters" to Mr. Odell and then rushed on their way. Mrs. Walker hung behind for only a moment to tell Mr. Odell once again how wonderful she thought his display truly was and then left to scramble more eggs.

In the quiet left behind on that lovely spring morning,

Mr. Odell stood at the door of the Regal and looked out at that tree. He couldn't be absolutely sure, but it sure seemed to him that there were more buds out than usual, pushing their way to the top.

Lamar

People around here are wack! Kicking up all that noise about nothing! There's nothing special about all that mess at the Regal. Nothing! The next person who gets in my face to tell me about it is going to hear out loud how wack they are! Yeah. They're going to hear it from me!

Old man Odell always trying to be the big man. Always has so much to say like he knows everything. Yeah. Okay, let's see how much old Mr. Big Man has to say after I get through. Yeah. Let's see what he'll be talking about then.

I'm through waiting for new tips. I'm not waiting for anything! Anyway I must be stupid for thinking I'll get new anything. I don't ever get nothing I want. Nothing, no time! Like on my birthday. Aunt Lou kept saying my moms was coming to bring me something. A gift for my birthday she said. Yeah. Some birthday that was. Moms never even showed up. She called up after midnight acting all sorry. I told her my birthday was over and to forget it. Yeah. That's what I told her.

I'll just go ahead and use what I already have. My can of red still has a lot of paint in it. So does the yellow. Wish I had more black. And silver. And new tips for sure. But wishing's not getting. Yeah. I know that.

Old man Odell is going to know it too. Yeah. He's going to know it good. I'm going to give him some heroes to look at. Yeah. Some REAL heroes. He'll be wishing his so-called heroes had been guarding that raggedy building to keep everything else away. But his wishing won't be getting either. Yeah.

Up until that late spring Saturday morning, things at the Regal had been kind of slow.

It wasn't that no one came to see the Retrospective, because some did. Especially the older people. Nana Rose came and brought some of her friends from church. A couple of them told their friends and those friends stopped by, too.

Little Catfish told his teacher about it and got permission to make an announcement to the class. After that his teacher said maybe she would arrange for a class trip to the Regal. But only after they did some research to learn more about some of the people whose pictures they would see there.

Roman asked his family to go with him to the Regal. "Maybe we'll go when I don't have so much to do," his father said. His older brother told Roman to tell him when the free movies started and he would go with Roman then.

Little Catfish asked Mr. Odell if they could print up some pages. "You know, like ones people hand out on the corner sometimes," he said.

"Fliers, you mean," Mr. Odell said. "Hmmmm. Maybe so. Let's think about what they might say."

Meanwhile, the big brass doors stayed open all day. The Retrospective sign still waved softly under the marquee even though it had gotten a little smudgy and torn in a couple of places. And some passersby continued to dribble in and out, now and then.

Until that Saturday morning.

As always, Mr. Odell was the first to get there. Pike Howard was with him. The barber had gotten in the habit of taking a morning walk to the Regal with his oldest friend. "It's good just to look around," he would say while the two of them wandered in the dimly lit space and remembered together.

"Now *that* man was a master entertainer," Pike Howard might say, looking up at the poster of Cab Calloway, the Hi De Ho Man dressed in his elegant white tails.

"No doubt about it," Mr. Odell would agree. Then he might look up at the poster of Lena Horne and smile. "And in her day, so was this gorgeous lady!" And, thinking of Little Catfish, he might add, "She was a good friend of Paul Robeson, you know. A *very* good friend."

Almost always the two would end up near the posters, pictures, and articles about Paul Robeson. The largest display of all. The one Little Catfish still headed for first every time he set foot inside the theater.

But on this Saturday morning the two men didn't even make it inside. What they saw on the front of the Regal stopped them.

It was impossible to tell what the ugly scrawls were supposed to be. Something in particular? Somebody? Several somebodies? If so, who? Maybe they were meant to be simply what they were: ugly slashes of red and yellow mixed in with filthy hiccups and blotches of black and silver. But no matter what it was *meant* to be, it had turned out as nothing more than a grand mess showing itself across the wide brass doors at the front of the Regal.

Such a shame it was to see. In their day these doors had been magnificent. Shimmering copper sentries, guarding the front of the theater. One of the prides of the Regal. And now . . . such a shame to see.

Pike Howard stood there, shaking his head from side to side. "Who on earth would want to do something like this? Especially now?"

Odell Davis hadn't moved either, and shook his head the same way. He had a few ideas about how Pike's questions might be answered but kept them to himself.

The two men were still standing like that when Little Catfish came running down the street. "Hey, everybody," he called. "Know what, Mr. Odell. I got a idea about the—" The rest of his words hung in the air. He had reached the two men and saw what they were looking at.

"The doors to our retrospective!" Little Catfish's words were a cry. "They're ruined!"

"Maybe not, maybe not," Mr. Odell said, not really believing himself.

Little Catfish's next thought made him shudder. "Is the inside messed up too?" he asked.

"I'll go check," Mr. Odell said, reaching for the familiar keys. "You wait here, little man."

But Little Catfish didn't wait. He followed Mr. Odell inside. So did Pike Howard. All three let out big breaths of relief when they saw that nothing inside had been bothered.

So there they stood. Each of them under the quiet ceiling of the Regal, looking up at the walls through the dim dusty light, then turning back again to see the doors and getting lost in their own thoughts.

Little Catfish felt the weight of unhappiness as he wondered why anybody would want to mess up what little they had in the neighborhood. "It's not fair," he finally mumbled. "It's just not fair!"

Pike Howard held himself back for a moment, then decided to let his thought go free. "'Fair' is a once-upon-a-time thing, little man," he said. "Something in fairy tales. In this life you got to make your own 'fair' happen."

Little Catfish's forehead wrinkled. "Huh?" he said.

Mr. Odell jumped in. "What Pike means is that a lot of the time, things turn out fair only when we *make* them turn out that way."

Seeing his young friend's scrunched-up face, Mr. Odell kept on, determined to make himself clear. "*We* have to take responsibility to make things turn out right, doing the best we can. 'Course, even then, nothing's promised, but it's still our best shot for making things fair." After a moment he quietly added, "Yep, in the long run, it's up to us!"

Of course, Odell Davis had believed this his whole life. But somehow, when he said the words out loud that day in the Regal . . . well, maybe on that particular day, in spite of everything that had happened, those words just sprouted wings and filled the air. The way determined words sometimes do.

Not knowing exactly what to do, Little Catfish and Mr. Odell just hung around. There was no use trying to clean up. Removing that mess was a job to be done by an expert. Someone who knew how to get rid of the paint without destroying the doors. So just being there like always was all the two friends really *could* do.

But instead of sitting outside as the spring breezes invited them to do, the two mostly stayed inside this particular day. Sometimes wandering around the lobby, examining favorite places. Other times just sitting together on that old leather sofa. Thinking. Wondering. And so they were when they heard the sounds of people approaching.

"Man, this is wack!" they heard one of them say. It was the voice of one of the big kids. The ones who hung out in the empty lot when the weather was friendly. Kids like Lamar.

Little Catfish sat up straighter without really realizing what he was doing. Now he saw the shadows of the boys. They were near the front of the doors.

"Messed up!" one of them said.

"Bet," another agreed.

Mr. Odell stood up and leaned sideways to make sure he could be seen and heard. "Don't stop there, gentlemen," he said. "Come on in and look around."

The boys looked at each other, not sure what they wanted to do. They had walked by only because somebody had told somebody else that "now there was really something special to see at the Regal." Word had gotten around that way.

Finally one of the boys wandered inside. Then the rest followed. Little Catfish looked at the line of big boys cautiously making their way inside. No Lamar. He got up from the sofa as Mr. Odell encouraged again. "Come on, come on in," he said, stretching out his hand. "Look around." And so they did.

"Hey, Mr. Odell," the self-appointed leader said. "This here's some strange wallpaper."

After the small chorus of laughter the boy had hoped for, he asked what he wanted to know. "Who's all these people? How come you put them up on the walls?"

"Happy you asked," Mr. Odell said. "And I'll be even happier to tell you."

Mr. Odell walked with the boys, pointing out things here and there. Adding bits and pieces of information he hoped would grab their attention.

You never heard of Oscar Micheaux? Why, he was the first person to make a movie that starred only black people. Yep, and this was in 1919!

Was William Pickett a *real* cowboy? I want you to know that Bill Pickett was one of the best! He invented the rodeo act of wrestling steers! You see it all the time in those old western movies. "Bulldogging," they called it. Yep, Bill Pickett made bulldogging famous.

Yep, this is the woman they made that TV movie about. Josephine Baker. She was real, all right, and a great entertainer. And yes, it's true that she moved to France to get away from the way black people were treated in America.

When they got to the collection of pictures and articles under "Our Tallest Tree," one of the boys called out, "How come there's so much about this dude? Who's he?"

It was Cheeks asking. Cheeks without Lamar for a change. Little Catfish peeked around the body in front of him to look at the taller-than-average buddy of Lamar. After a thoughtful moment he stepped out from where he had been behind the group. "That's Mr. Paul Robeson," he said. Even to him his voice sounded little. He decided to say it again. "Paul Robeson" came his louder voice with a bit more courage added. "And there's a whole bunch of things about him to tell."

That was all Little Catfish could get out right then. In the following silence the boys looked up at the display. The largest one of all in the lobby.

"Looks like he was some kind of football player," one said. "But check out that wack uniform he's wearing."

"Look here. My man played basketball, too," another said.

"And baseball!" said a third. "See? Look over there."

Cheeks moved closer to the wall to look at the pictures. "Naw," he said, looking up and down the display. "All these ain't the same man. Ain't *nobody* all that."

Cheeks's words rang in Little Catfish's ears. They were the same words he had said to Mr. Odell all those months ago. Almost the exact same ones.

The ringing words gave him extra courage. He moved forward to stand directly under the display. To a spot in front of Cheeks. "It *is* the same man," he said. His voice was little again, but he kept talking. "In *all* these pictures." The voice got bigger. "The articles, too." Bigger still. "Look real good and you can see for yourself." Little Catfish began feeling proud of how his voice sounded. "His name was Mr. Paul Leroy Robeson. He was all that and a whole lot more!"

Gathering his whole supply of built-up courage, Little Catfish pointed his finger up at the largest picture and kept going.

**He was good at ALL these sports. Plus,
track. In football he even played for the pros!**

After a few moments it was as if a younger and shorter version of Mr. Odell had taken over.

**That's Mr. Paul Robeson with his Phi Beta
Kappa key. That's something you get when
you go to college and get the best grades they
can give! Know what else? He spoke a whole
bunch of languages—maybe even twenty!**

As the group inched its way along the wall, a big smile planted itself on Mr. Odell's face. A smile that grew big enough to make its way to his heart as he stood there watching and listening.

Yup, Mr. Paul Robeson was a singer *and* actor. He acted in a bunch of movies. He didn't think most of the movies were all that great, though. Mostly because of how the people who made them wanted black people to be like.

Satisfied with the way things were going, Mr. Odell made his way back to the opened doors. Something he had done several times that morning. He looked up the sidewalk in one direction and then the other. Also as he had done several times earlier. Still no Lamar. Nowhere in sight.

Perhaps he should try to find out where Lamar was. One of the young men inside would probably know. Especially the one called Cheeks. The one who seemed to consider Lamar a hero of sorts.

Mr. Odell turned to look at the group of boys and wondered what he should do. Things were going so well. The boys acted like they were interested in what they were seeing and hearing. Even asking a few questions now and then. At least, that's how it seemed.

Yep, things were going better than he would have imagined. Might asking about the missing Lamar move their thinking in a different direction?

The wonderings raced through Mr. Odell's mind. Maybe he should call Cheeks aside. Yes, he could do that and quietly ask him about his buddy. But would Cheeks understand why Mr. Odell wanted to know? Would any of them understand? Would they believe it wasn't really about the doors?

Odell Davis quietly leaned back against the corner of the opened doors. Maybe he should just wait until Lamar came along. He would sooner or later. He always did. Like most of the men-becoming around there, Lamar had no place else much to go.

Lamar

I'll show them! All of them. Know-nothings who been saying how whoever was trying to be a door artist at the Regal must have had a crazy spell or something. All them laughing, thinking I don't know who they were talking about. Even Cheeks. Laughing like the rest of them while they stand around signifying. None of them big enough to say anything to my face but I know what's on their minds. Yeah. I know.

Now I'm through waiting. I'm not waiting another day! There's stacks of spray cans in Foley's Hardware over on Eighth Street. Yeah. I'll go in there when it's crowded and pick up a couple. Then I'll go back and get a couple more. Yeah. And nobody's going to stop me. Nobody!

When I finish this time all those fools going to be singing a different tune. Yeah. Real different. Folks been coming to that trashy old building to see a bunch of wack junk. But I'm going to give them something worth looking at. Yeah! Something for real.

Old man Odell was waving at me from across the street the other day. Acting like he wanted me to come over there. Like he had something to say to me. Yeah. But I'm not interested in any of his jive talk. He doesn't care what's in my head so how come I should care what's in his? All any of those old dudes ever want to say is how wrong we are. Yeah. That's all that ever comes out of their mouths.

Maybe after I finish this time I'll mosey on over there. Like I'm just passing by. I can check out for myself what folks are saying. Yeah. Old man Odell can tell me then what's on his mind. Then he'll really have something to talk about. Yeah.

Mr. Odell was alone when he arrived at the Regal that next Wednesday morning. No one was with him under the drizzling skies to see the newly made slashes of paint on the doors. And on the outer walls of the building. And splattered on the sidewalk along the front. No one was there to see Odell Davis's head going slowly from side to side as he looked at what had been done. No one to hear the small almost-cry of sadness that snaked out of his mouth as his eyes digested all that ugliness.

This time the sprayed-on colors were sharp. Bold. But what they were meant to represent still wasn't clear. Mostly because of the uneven slashes that had been thrown up the first time. The new whatever-it-was-supposed-to-be had been painted over the old whatever-it-had-been. If the new had been made on a plain, colorless surface, maybe then there would have been more of something to see. But as it was . . .

All in all, it was a grand mess. Now more than ever.

Mr. Odell was in the same spot when Billy Bradshaw drove by. Billy was on his way to his drop off a few groceries to his Auntie Evelyn and saw his old friend standing there. Stuck in one spot and getting drenched while the rain began to pour.

Billy stopped, rolled down his car window, and called out, "Mr. O.! You okay? Everything all right?" Without waiting for an answer, he pulled his car to the curb and jumped out. "Mr. O.?" he called again, running to get close to the old man. When he got there, he realized that everything wasn't all right. Far from it.

Billy had been a frequent visitor at the Regal since that

first day. He was in Pike Howard's chair for his regular appointment the first time word about the Retrospective had made its way down the street. He and the barber had rushed together to the old theater to see what all the fuss was about. Billy loved what he had seen. Even more, he loved the idea of what Mr. Odell was hoping to do.

"Go on, Mr. O.!" Billy B. had said, pumping Mr. Odell's right hand up and down. "Helping us to remember our heroes! Man, this is something *else!*"

Now, seeing what somebody else was trying to do—perhaps even someone from the community—Billy was shocked. Hurt. Mad.

Mr. Odell couldn't make out exactly what it was that Billy Bradshaw said when he stopped beside him. But he knew that the younger man's feelings were a mirror of his own.

Getting wetter by the second, Billy pulled at Mr. Odell's arm. "Come on, Mr. O.," he said, gently nudging the older man toward the locked doors, "let's get out of this rain." And only then, when they moved forward, did they realize that one of the used-to-be-bronze doors was ajar.

Using his left hand while his right automatically reached for the keys, Mr. Odell slowly pushed open the door. Billy moved closely behind him. Without being aware of what they were doing, both men took in and held a deep breath as the door swung into the darkened space.

On sunny days one could get a view of the inside just after the doors opened. Even before Mr. Odell flicked the switch that turned on the semicircle of hidden lights around the edges of the ceiling. But on this day there was no sunlight to spill inside. There was only darkness. And fear of what the light might bring.

After a long quiet moment, Billy did what Mr. Odell couldn't bring himself to do. Billy B. went over to the box on the wall just behind the old ticket counter and turned on the lights.

In the next long quiet moments, the two stood side by side, taking it all in. The hateful slashes of color criss-crossing the carpet. From front to back, corner to corner. The figure that had been started in the center and then left unfinished. The angry blotches of color making their way up one of the walls and then mysteriously stopping. But only after ruining one of the displays.

All in all, a grand, terrible mess.

Mr. Odell could find no words. His shoulders slumped under the weight of all the unsaid he was keeping inside.

Billy Bradshaw looked at his old friend and saw the sadness. The growing defeat in a man who had helped guide his childhood. Seeing this, a fury begain to build like a fire inside him. It pushed up his shoulders and balled up his hands. After a few tense seconds more, it exploded from his mouth. "That's it! No more! This must end. This *will* end!"

Odell Davis, almost wrecked by what was in front of him, turned to Billy without understanding.

When Billy spoke again, he commanded his voice to be calm. Almost gentle. "All this senseless vandalism, Mr. O.," he said, his eyes still blazing above the softened voice. "It's going to stop. It's over. Finished."

How you figure that, Billy? How you going to stop something you don't even see coming? How you going to make people start protecting what they got when they don't believe it's worth protecting? These questions rushed through Mr. Odell's mind, adding to his weight of sadness. Yet he stood there still silent.

But the questions had been in Billy's mind also. They'd been there since the first time someone had vandalized the Regal. He had thought about them again and again. He couldn't be sure he had come up with the right answers, but he had definitely come up with a plan. Now it was time to say something about his plan out loud.

"It's over, Mr. O., because *we're* going to end it our-selves," Billy said. He put his arm around Mr. Odell's shoulders and pulled him along. Turned him away from the sight of all that anger turned loose on the walls and floor. "*We're* going to take control."

He walked Mr. Odell to the door. Toward the pitiful streaks of sunlight trying to peek through the gray skies. "We're going to get the word out and get people involved."

Mr. Odell looked at Billy. The sadness in his eyes was hardened by the frown on his face. "Who, Billy?" he said, challenging. "Who we going to get involved? Who *wants* to be involved?"

Billy B. chuckled. A small laugh of hope. "You'd be sur-prised, I think," he said.

By the time they reached the door, the rain had stopped. "Looks like the heavens ain't crying no more, Mr. O.," Billy said, looking up and hoping Mr. Odell would do the same. Turn his eyes away from the ugly marks beneath them. "The gray skies are moving on." After a second he added, "I say we do the same."

"What *are* you suggesting we do, Billy?" Mr. Odell said. He looked directly into the younger man's eyes, his own eyes showing the beginnings of a new concentration.

"It's just like I said: We going to get people involved!" Billy threw his arm around Mr. Odell's shoulders. Straighter, pushed-back shoulders. "And the first person is going to be Cleveland Tolbert. Remember him?"

Looking up at the sky, Mr. Odell searched his memory. "Oh, yeah," he said after a moment. "Cleveland. One of your running buddies. A little dude. Always nosing around, asking questions. Getting into folks' business." Mr. Odell smiled. "Yeah, I remember him."

Billy returned the smile. "That little dude is now a big dude down at the *City Gazette*," he said.

"You don't say!" Mr. Odell's face brightened with surprise.

"I do say," Billy said, grinning. "Cleveland's nose for news paid off. I think hearing about the current goings-on at the Regal will give my man's nose a real good itch for him to scratch."

The two men kept standing there in the messed-up entrance of the weary old Regal. Talking. Tossing around ideas. One can only wonder if either of them noticed the path of bright blue beginning to make its way across the sky. Or whether they were aware of the sweet smell of blossoms drifting from that bursting-out-all-over tree.

Little Catfish

Mama says her favorite part of the newspaper article is where they give my name. She reads that part out loud so much I know it by heart. "Among the Regal's displays is an impressive collection of information about Paul Robeson, one of the most gifted men of modern times. My tour guide through this collection was young Mr. Douglass Walker, an outstanding third grader who shows himself to be quite a Robeson expert.'"

I like that part a lot too. A whole lot. But I wish that newspaper man had used my other name. Then everybody would know for sure who he was talking about.

Nana Rose says her favorite part is where they tell people to write letters. Like to the aldermen and the mayor. She says she's going to get all the ladies she makes quilts with to write and that she's going to write a bunch of letters herself. Nana Rose will too. She always does what she says she's going to.

My favorite part is the whole entire article. Mr. O. says that's his favorite part too. He talks a lot about the part that tells how the Regal is a historical landmark or something. But he still says every single word in that article is his favorite part.

When we talked about it the night Mr. Odell came over for dinner, Mama and Nana Rose said a whole something can't be a favorite part. Mr. Odell and me both said yes it can. Then Mr. O. pointed to me and said that he bet all of them agree that the whole of this young man (he meant me) is a favorite part of our universe. Mama and Nana Rose said well, they guess they had to change what they had been thinking!

It was so much fun that night. We mostly just sat around talking, but it was still fun. Mostly it was Nana Rose and

Mr. O. who had stuff to tell about, but everybody had something to say. Me too.

    It was like we were a family.

Some of the time while we were talking about how things could get better, Mr. O. got this look on his face. I think he's worrying about more stuff happening. I worry about that too, but not as much as I did at first. Maybe because I haven't seen Lamar around. Not for a long time.

    I know it's bad to wish that anybody is gone for good. But I think it's okay to hope that anything that keeps things from being better will kind of stay gone.

The Sunday after the newspaper article came out in the *City Gazette*, Mr. Odell got up especially early. He had set his mind on something and wanted it done before he went to church. He dressed in his dark blue suit and yellow striped tie, ate a fast breakfast, and got on his way.

Under a cloudless sky Mr. Odell kept his brisk, steady pace until he reached Ninth Avenue. The street where Mrs. Louise Thomas lived. The woman who, according to Cheeks, Lamar lived with and called Aunt Lou.

"It's number one eighteen on Ninth Avenue," Cheeks had said. "But I think Lamar's gone from around there. At least that's what people been saying." Mr. Odell waited to see if Cheeks would supply more information. He didn't. Mr. Odell wanted to ask more questions, but, well, he didn't. No use putting Cheeks on the spot. Or making him think he was.

Now, having reached Ninth Avenue, the jumble of feelings Mr. Odell had been carrying for weeks slowed him down. What would be the best way to approach Lamar? How could he get him to listen? *Really* listen. Could he help Lamar believe that the messed-up center wasn't really the issue? Was *Lamar* the one responsible for it? Even though Mr. Odell believed deep inside himself that Lamar was, he had no real proof. Since helping Lamar was what mattered, should the vandalism even be part of the conversation?

But what if he couldn't have *any* conversation with Lamar? What if it was like Cheeks said? What if Lamar was gone?

This was the question that troubled him the most. If

Lamar were gone, how was Mr. Odell going to be able to forgive himself?

Walking slower and slower, Odell Davis finally reached the building. He climbed up the seven steps leading to 118 and pushed the doorbell button. No sound. He pushed it again. Again no sound. So, he knocked on the door once, then knocked again, harder.

Standing there on the stoop, Mr. Odell saw the window curtain being pushed back from inside. He stepped back from the door so that whoever was looking out could see him. Then he waited. After another moment the door opened, but only the inches the still-attached chain latch allowed.

"Yes?" came the voice from inside. A woman's voice.

Mr. Odell moved close to the opened space. "Mrs. Thomas?" he asked, peering inside.

The face was in the shadows. "Yes?" came the voice again.

"Mrs. Thomas, my name is Odell Davis and I . . . " He wasn't quite sure how to finish. He was what? A friend of Lamar's? Mr. Odell started again. "I'm looking for Lamar. I know him from the, um, the community center. The place that used to be the Regal."

"Just a moment," the woman said. She pushed the door forward to unlatch it, then opened it all the way. "I'm sorry, Mr., ah, Mr. . . . what you say your name was?" The woman's eyes were watchful.

"Davis," said Mr. Odell, speaking directly to her eyes. "Odell Davis. I don't mean to bother you, Mrs. Thomas. I want a chance to talk with Lamar. Just to speak with him."

The face looking back at him was kind. "I'm sorry, Mr. Davis," Mrs. Thomas said, "but Lamar's not here. Lamar . . . well, he's gone. He doesn't live here anymore."

Where is he? Why did he move away? Has he left to live with someone else? Did someone take him away?

The questions ran through Mr. Odell's mind as he stood there only inches away from someone who could probably tell him the answers. But he didn't know if he should ask. If he had a right to.

It was as if the watchful eyes saw behind Mr. Odell's quiet face. "Mr. Davis," Mrs. Thomas started as the sound of young children's voices somewhere in the house interrupted. She looked behind her, then continued. "This is a foster home. I keep several children here. When one of the older kids starts acting . . . you know, like they know everything, like they're grown, it causes trouble."

A child inside yelled, "Give it back! It's mine!"

Mrs. Thomas rubbed her hand along her cheek. "When children get to be too much for me to handle, I can't keep them here," she said. She sighed. Her voice got sadder. "Especially a kid like Lamar. A kid who doesn't know anything about his dad, and has a mom who . . . well, she has her own troubles."

Another sigh. "Lamar started acting out. Like he was mad at the world. He was starting getting into serious trouble."

In the silence, the fussing child could be heard again, now laughing.

"Do you know where Lamar is, Mrs. Thomas?" Mr. Odell asked, finally.

"I don't," Mrs. Thomas said. Her eyes dropped. "People from Youth Services picked him up. They said something about a group home." Her head dropped as her eyes had, but her voice rushed on. "I worry that Lamar may even have to spend time in juvie."

Juvie. A jail for kids.

The two adults stood there in the doorway. The one who had tried in her way to help Lamar. The other who in his way had waited too long to try.

After that there was nothing left to say. Mr. Odell thanked Mrs. Thomas for speaking with him, tipped his

Sunday-only hat, and turned to go on his way.

Slowly, Mr. Odell retraced his steps, going back the way he came. His questions weren't slowing him down this time. His footsteps dragged because of his heavy heart.

It rained a lot that spring. Hard, driving rain that makes fierce *kerplunk* sounds so loud on the windows you start thinking maybe something is trying to get inside. Of course, inside is the place to be in that kind of weather. Especially when you're eight and it's early on a gray, crying morning, you're a little sleepy, and the rain boots your grandmother insists you wear are not the cool kind with lots of colors. Like the ones in the advertisements showing kids splashing through puddles.

Little Catfish looked down at the lumpy, mud-splattered boots by the door. "Aw, Nana Rose," he complained, "those boots ain't no good. My feet still get wet when I wear them."

Nana Rose answered without looking up from the quilt square she was working on. "Those boots *are* good," she said. "They *are* better than nothing. Stop wasting time and put them on."

Pouting, Little Catfish dropped to the floor and started jerking on the boots. "It's been raining for a quintillion days. How come it has to rain so much anyway?" he mumbled.

"Don't begrudge us the rain, grandson," Nana Rose said, stretching a long piece of red thread into the air. "That rain helps clear out the old. It brings newness. Brings it to the earth, to the plants, even to the streets . . ."

Little Catfish wasn't paying much attention to what Nana Rose was saying. He hadn't stopped listening on purpose; all of his concentration was on the battle he was having with the left boot. The heel of his shoe always got caught in that place where the lining was ripped.

Anyway, Nana Rose wasn't saying anything her grandson hadn't heard before. Many times. How things were getting ready to change. For the better. How sure she was this was so.

"I can feel it, grandson. I can feel it in my bones," she said while, half-listening, Little Catfish struggled with that stubborn left boot.

Little Catfish's struggle wasn't the only one taking place that gray, damp morning. Down the street behind the splattered doors, Odell Davis was in a battle of his own.

Unlike Little Catfish, who hadn't wanted any part of the worn-out boots, Mr. Odell had gotten into his struggle on purpose. He had taken time to search through the dozen or so boxes piled on his closet shelf to find a few sheets of letter-writing paper. He had gone out of his way to get to the new pharmacy store on Eighth Street to buy the envelopes he thought would have been in the box along with the paper but hadn't. Then he had doubled back to the corner store to buy stamps from the machine there.

Now he faced the most difficult part of the struggle: deciding exactly what to write. Knowing what to say in the first letter wouldn't be hard. The tricky part of that letter had been getting the name of the person at Youth Services who should get it. But Billy Bradshaw had helped him solve that problem.

"Maxi Teal," Billy had said, writing down the address on a scrap of paper. "Auntie Evelyn knows her from other work the lady has done around here and can probably help you out. Ms. Teal is very caring, Auntie Evelyn says, and will do what she can. If she doesn't have the information herself, she'll put you in touch with someone who does."

That wasn't the only help Billy B. offered. "The Internet's probably the quickest way to get in touch with Ms. Teal," he said. "I'm sure we can track her down through the Youth Services website."

Mr. Odell had looked at Billy, smiling. "Thanks, Billy B.," he said. "I appreciate your help, man, but I don't know nothing about that Internet stuff. That's something for you young folks."

"Now you sounding like Auntie Evelyn," Billy said, shaking his head and chuckling. "Trust me, Mr. O., there's nothing to it. A couple of clicks here and there and you'll be right where you need to be."

"I'm right where I'm supposed to be now, Billy B.," Mr. O. answered. "You gave me the information I needed. Anyway, I need to send something to the Youth Services lady, and I can't do that through no Internet."

"Don't be too sure about that, Mr. O.," Billy B. had said.

But Mr. Odell was sure. There was a second letter he had to write. It would be sealed and enclosed with the first. And both of them would be sent directly to Ms. Maxi Teal through what Billy B. had called "snail mail"— the post office.

What Mr. Odell wasn't sure about—what he was

struggling over—was what to write in that second letter. He wasn't sure about that at all.

What do I say in a letter to a young blood who hardly even talked to me? Who acted like he didn't want to hear anything I had to say? What do I say to make him listen? To make him know I really care that he does?

The questions went around and around in Mr. Odell's mind like a merry-go-round of words. Standing there at the old ticket counter with the letter-writing paper in front of him and a ballpoint in his hand, he kept looking up at the crowded walls around him. Maybe he was hoping that one of his heroes would help him get some answers.

It was going to be a struggle, but Mr. Odell was determined to see it through. Just like Little Catfish had finally pulled on that stubborn left boot, Odell Davis was going to get that second letter written. To Lamar.

Two Mondays after the newspaper article appeared and one Monday after Mr. Odell finally mailed his two-in-one letter, people from the Restoration Society came around. They wanted to check out the Regal for themselves. Get a good look at the historic landmark and see if they might help.

Sugar Johnson saw them drive up and park in front of the Regal. It was a little after noon. Mr. Odell had gone to get a bite to eat at Nelson's. Not wanting them to leave without talking to anybody, Sugar Johnson called out from her stoop. "Odell'll be back in a minute or two," she said. "He don't stay away from the Regal too long for anything."

Little Catfish had gone to Nelson's with Mr. Odell that day. An in-service day for teachers, and no school for kids. The two of them were still together when they got back to the old theater. After finding out who the people standing by the big gray car parked right in front of the Regal were, Mr. Odell and Little Catfish invited the group inside.

"They were in there for the longest," Sugar Johnson said to her neighbor Lilia Terry, who lately was getting to be a stoop-sitter herself. "I bet those people got the grand tour. You know, Odell and Little Catfish showing off everything."

Sugar Johnson would have won that bet. Mr. Odell and Little Catfish spent over an hour with the Restoration Society people—a group whose business was to make valuable old things like new again. After seeing the inside of the Regal and hearing what Odell Davis and Little Catfish had to say, the group was anxious to offer its help.

"We can use our resources to restore the brass doors to their original condition," said the person leading the group. The woman Little Catfish tried not to look at when she talked. Her mouth reminded him of the goldfish in his classroom. The way that tiny orange mouth puckered, blowing air bubbles in the tank. Looking at the woman made it hard for Little Catfish not to giggle.

"We can also help reinforce the inside walls to make them as they were when the Regal was built," she said. "Your displays will be much safer on improved and stronger walls."

Mr. Odell said their help would be greatly appreciated. "But only if some of our older boys can work along with you," he said. "We want them to have an understanding of how that kind of work is done."

"Oh, certainly, certainly," said the woman.

Little Catfish grinned, saying in his head, "Okay, Miss Goldfish."

* * *

A day after the Restoration Society people had been there, students from the art school at the university came by to volunteer their services. This group was led by a young man whose father had lived in the neighborhood years ago.

"Dad lives in the islands now," the young man said. Carson. "I e-mailed the newspaper article to him and he wrote back asking to see if there was anything I could do to help."

After Mr. Odell and Little Catfish gave the students the grand tour, Carson had an idea. "You know, we can help with those displays," he said. "Like painting backgrounds, doing framing. Arrangement. Things like that."

"That would be great," Mr. Odell agreed.

"Hey, I got a idea about another something," Little Catfish said. "Wanna hear it?"

Carson grinned. "We sure do, little man," he said.

Little Catfish's voice sang with excitement. "Me and my friend Roman and some other kids want to paint a mural on the outside." He saw Mr. Odell's eyes look away as he kept on. "You know, something to . . . ah . . ." Little Catfish stopped, not knowing how to put his idea into words that wouldn't stir the bad memories. Words that wouldn't hurt.

Mr. Odell stepped in. "I think the little man here is saying that we need something new on the outside walls to cover up something old. Something started by mistake."

Little Catfish looked into Mr. Odell's face, then grinned. "Yeah," he said. "That's what we need."

"There's help we can give in that area, too," Carson said. "You need scaffolding to paint a really good mural. We can build it. And if you want, we can also teach you guys some cool techniques in doing murals. Interested?"

"Yeah, real interested," Little Catfish said, almost dancing with excitement. Then, with a bright twinkle in his eyes, he looked at Carson. "If you got any spare paint, we'll be interested in that, too!"

While the art students began the scaffolding—the layers of planks and steps the kids could stand and sit on while they painted—Little Catfish and his friends worked on the paper sketch of the picture they wanted to paint. After watching for a while, Mr. Odell called to his young friend.

"Whatchu want, Mr. O.?" Little Catfish could hardly put his mind on anything but that big picture he and his buddies would be painting.

"Just a little something," Mr. Odell said, and put his arm around Little Catfish's shoulders to draw him close.

Little Catfish forced his excited feet to stop dancing around, looked up into Mr. O.'s face, and waited.

"Just this." Odell Davis spoke slowly, making sure the words would be right. "I think it would be a good idea to leave an empty space somewhere in that mural."

Little Catfish's face showed that he didn't quite under-stand.

Mr. Odell made sure their eyes were connecting. "A space for adding something later," he said. "You never know. Maybe you'll think of something else that should be in the picture."

Little Catfish looked over at the rows of horizontal and vertical boards slowly making their way up in front of the outside wall of the building and hunched his shoulders. "I guess," he said in a voice not sure but will-ing. "Okay, Mr. O."

Mr. Odell watched Little Catfish hurry back to the group. "You never know, he said softly. "Maybe one day someone will come around to add their own something special to the picture. Yep, you never know."

Lamar

This is wack! Old man Odell writing me a letter. Wack!

Maxi brought me the letter, talking about having something special for me. Yeah. Something special all right. Good thing I didn't start expecting something like that time when the package came from Aunt Lou. Wasn't anything but a bunch of shirts and socks. Stuff she said she hoped I could use. Aunt Lou just trying to be nice, but there wasn't nothing special in that package for me. Just like in this letter.

Maxi says she wants her and me to go out some Saturdays. She's a okay lady most of the time. Like telling me to call her just Maxi. Not Miss or nothing like that. But now she probably cooking up something with that plan and thinking she being slick. Yeah. She probably got something hooked up with old man Odell. Yeah. The two of them setting me up.

Old man Odell thinking he slick too. Trying to get me in his territory so he can dis me. Yeah. That's his plan. That's what he seemed to be doing all the time when I was around there.

Maybe one of these times when nobody's expecting anything, I just might show up. Yeah, right out of the blue. Maybe I'll even get right up in old man Odell's face. I'll say here I am, so what you want. Yeah. I'll show him I'm not scared of being around there. Yeah. That's what I'll do. One of these days.

Cleveland Tolbert's first article in the *City Gazette* got such a good response from readers (readers wrote more than a hundred letters!) that the editor asked him to do a series of articles about the goings-on at the Regal. These articles brought people from everywhere to see for themselves what was happening. At first it was mostly people from around the neighborhood who came. Those who hadn't bothered during the first days of the retrospective. Gradually these neighborhood visitors were joined by people from nearby neighborhoods. Then by those in far-away parts of the city.

The day Mrs. Taylor-Jones from the New Bethel

A.M.E. came to see the exhibits, she brought more than friends with her. "Mr. Robeson was one of our greatest civil rights fighters, you know," she said to Mr. Odell. Then she handed over a bag of what she called "legitimate Paul Robeson treasures."

"There's an autographed copy in here of *Here I Stand*," she said in her quiet, careful voice. "The book Paul Robeson wrote about his life. There's also a photograph that my late husband took of Mr. Robeson at a protest rally."

Then, with a small smile, she leaned closer to Mr. Odell. "I am hoping, Mr. Davis," she said softly, "that you will want to make these things a small part of your lovely display. It would be so gratifying to me to see them when I come for our church concert which we hope to hold here this summer."

Mrs. Taylor-Jones's gifts weren't the only treasures on display at the Regal. A new glass case donated by the

Johnson Cabinet Company held an impressive collection of memorabilia. It was next to the restored ticket counter whose gold cagelike front was the place to sell or pick up tickets for one of the events now being held there. Included in the display were two original programs given to the audience that long-ago day when the poet Countee Cullen read his famous sonnet at the Regal; a sheet of music from one of Duke Ellington's compositions, signed by the composer, of course; and a picture of the movie stars Ossie Davis and Harry Belafonte standing on either side of Paul Robeson.

When Little Catfish saw this photograph for the first time, he asked Mr. Odell about his photograph with Paul Robeson.

"Which one's that?" Mr. Odell wanted to know.

"You know," Little Catfish reminded. "The one you said was taken under the tree that time."

"Oh, I'm saving that for a while," Mr. Odell said. "I'll

bring it in to stir up interest when things start to slow down." Then he winked at Little Catfish. "Yep, that's the plan."

Well, things didn't slow down. They just kept getting better. And busier. RETROSPECTIVE AT THE REGAL. That's how the sign read between the new skipping square of lights around the repaired marquee Billy Bradshaw had taken responsibility for.

Billy B. also donated speakers. "The Regal's getting the best woofers and tweeters on the market," he said to Mr. Odell when he installed the speakers. Soon Mr. Odell's collection of old records, now transferred to disc, could be heard throughout the lobby. The new sound system and improved wiring in the main auditorium also made the sound of the free films much better.

"It's good advertisement for the shop," Billy said, talking about the new Bradshaw's Electronics shop that was opening soon down the street. It would be in the same building that now had an Internet cafe. There were only two computers in the narrow space so far, but it was a start.

The sound system did indeed spice up presentation of the films Mr. Odell started showing. But the films themselves weren't exactly what the kids had been expecting. There were no action or adventure stories. No stories much at all except for the Oscar Micheaux films Pike Howard tracked down and donated to the Regal. Most of the other films were documentaries. Like the one Little Catfish sat through at least three times: *Paul Robeson: Here I Stand.* People came to see the films, but usually not enough came at any one time to fill up the auditorium.

But that too changed the weekend of the African-American Storytellers Festival.

Tellers from around the country were planning to be

at the festival. The organizers had planned for it to take place in one of the theaters downtown, but when the tellers heard what was happening at the Regal, they insisted that it take place there.

The Saturday of the festival Mr. Odell arrived at his usual time to unlock the doors (for crowd control, he felt only one should be left open). The first telling session wasn't going to begin until two o'clock in the afternoon, but until that time the regularly scheduled events would go on as usual. Like the weaving and pottery and puppet-making classes held every Saturday. In addition, one of the most famous of the tellers was presenting a special "Tell *Your* Story" class for the community. Mr. Odell hoped that everybody coming to the classes would stick around for the beginning of the festival. He hoped for a huge crowd to fill the Regal on this special day.

Well, Mr. Odell got everything he hoped for that bright summer Saturday. That and a whole lot more.

People started arriving for the festival around eleven. A few had come for the storytelling class, but most came early to have a chance to look around at everything before the activities started. And maybe have a bite to eat at that fish place they had heard about.

By twelve thirty there was a line building up outside the theater. Not the long line that was there by one o'clock, but a line nonetheless. Part of the twelve-thirty line was there because of the fliers Little Catfish and Roman and some of their classmates were handing out up and down the street. They had made more than one hundred fliers in school that Friday and were determined to hand out every single one.

"Jambo!" Little Catfish would call to people passing, using the Swahili greeting he had learned at the center. "Come to the storytelling festival! Learn about some of our heroes while you're there!"

Close to one thirty, when the storytellers and their musicians began arriving in their beautiful, billowing robes, the line extended almost to the corner. The oohs and ahhs of the crowd watching the entertainers step from their cars and stroll to the entrance of the Regal stretched even farther.

Mr. Odell had stationed himself by the door so he could welcome everybody. Personally touch every hand he could. His welcoming smile wrote the thoughts of his heart across his face. "What a grand day this is," it said. "What a truly grand day!"

The crowd was still building when Mr. Odell spotted a face that made his smile flicker. Then it brightened and grew even wider. The familiar face of the young man moving toward him still had that look of defiance. Of doubt and challenge. But around the face was a hopeful difference. The hair above it was newly twisted; the sweater and jeans below it hung neatly on the sturdy, though still slouching frame.

It was a soft, unfamiliar voice that Mr. Odell heard when the boy got close enough to speak to him directly. The surprise of it made the old man's head spin. "I think you must be Mr. Odell," the voice said.

Mr. Odell could do no more than nod his head at the speaker. The woman who was with the boy. She held out her hand. "I'm Maxi Teal, Mr. Odell. I'm very happy to meet you."

"And I'm very happy to meet you," Mr. Odell said, stretching out his right hand. "Very happy indeed."

"My young friend and I often spend Saturdays together, catching up on things around town," Maxi Teal said in her cheerful voice. "I finally convinced him that this Saturday there would be no better place to be than here!"

"I'm glad you did, Miss Maxi Teal," Mr. Odell said, trying hard to will the eyes of the young man to look at him. Eyes that seemed to be focusing on everything else but him.

From the time Maxi Teal and the boy had gotten out of her car, now parked almost three blocks away, the young man had been unable to pull his eyes away from sights he almost could not believe.

How could this be the street on which he had spent so many hours? The blocks he and Cheeks and some of the other posse regulars had roamed day and sometimes night? The street on which he once said had never shown him anything beautiful?

Of course, some things were the same as they always had been. Like Coffey Miller's really ugly bulldog sitting as usual in the window of Coffey's second-floor apartment. That chicken dog would bark at every person who passed by that window, but run to hide under the bed if it heard anybody coming up the stairs.

But so many, many things were different. Like the new

coats of paint on the row of buildings where the corner store and newsstand were. And the new awning over the barbershop right across the street. (Of course, that wasn't all that surprising; Pike Howard always kept his place up.)

But wait. Could that be Hambone Kelly making his way down the street? Dressed in a buttoned-up shirt and walking without even a hint of weaving? Stopping to tip his old army cap to Miss Verdell when she passed by him on the sidewalk?

The closer the boy and Miss Maxi got to the Regal, the more amazed he became.

Old Maurice standing there on the sidewalk with a *real* saxophone in his hand. *And* playing so lively you could hear it a block away. It sounded like that song you could hear old Maurice humming—if you got close enough and bothered to listen. Who knew old Maurice could really play!

The boy's eyes shone with disbelief when he saw the

long, sleek black limousine pull up to the entrance of the old theater. Who were all those people getting out, dressed in such brilliant colors? What business did they have on this street?

Now, slowly making their way, the woman and boy reached the edge of the crowd. They were close enough to finally see the front of the building. The whole of it. The doors. The mural.

The boy stopped, unable for a moment to make his feet go farther. He became rooted by the deep shame that rushed through his veins. At the same time he could feel the warmth of a certain joyful surprise.

Those doors. Not splattered, not dented or scratched. Not anything but tall, bronze, and beautiful. As was the mural. Its vibrant colors and sweeping strokes covered both walls on either side. It was fantastic—even with that strange empty space near the edge of one side. But who were those people it showed? It looked like versions of one person. One black man. Could that be?

The whole of it was almost more than he could take in. Then came a not-recently-heard-but-familiar voice.

"Hey there, young man."

It was Mr. Odell. Greeting the young man-becoming with his voice, having decided to wait until another time to throw an arm of welcome around those sloping shoulders. Then he extended his right hand once again and said, "I'm glad you're here. It's good to see you."

For a moment the boy struggled with the smile he could feel pushing at his cheeks. Then, slowly, he gave it up.

Lamar.

What a difference there was on the street that very next summer. . . .

A new clothes shop had opened. It didn't have as many fancy outfits as the Quality Shop had displayed in its heyday, but what was there was good. At least, Little Catfish's mama thought so.

"No reason to go all the way downtown, baby," she said when Little Catfish asked about getting new jeans to replace the ones he had torn playing baseball at the new field. "We can get them right down the street."

A big sign on the corner promised that a new supermarket would be coming soon. In the meantime, the greengrocer that had taken over two vacant stores in the middle of the block was doing a great business, offering fresh, plump fruits and vegetables.

HIRING SOON signs were posted everywhere around the old bakery, but nobody knew exactly what the jobs were going to be, or what the building would be turned into. All the entrances were still boarded up except the door the workers used at the back to go in and out. All the windows had been replaced but were taped over with newspaper. Drilling, sawing, and hammering noises sang from inside the entire workday.

For Sugar Johnson, there was simply *too* much going on. She told her friend Lilia, who had added pots of geraniums to her newly painted stoop, that all the busyness and noise gave her headaches. "Humph! Can't hardly sit outside at all," Sugar Johnson grumbled. "Got to stay in my kitchen to have peace and quiet. Humph!"

The day the city planted the rows of new trees, the

traffic jam caused by the flatbed trucks and work crews didn't clear up until after dark. Just about everybody was talking about it over dinner that evening at Nelson's, which now stayed open until midnight every night. Except on Mondays when Mr. Nelson took his wife out to dinner.

So, as things turned out, that old tree isn't the only tree on the street any more. It's just the tallest.

Paul Robeson: The Tallest Tree

On his forty-sixth birthday, there was a huge celebration for Paul Robeson. More than eight thousand people gathered to honor him, among them family, friends, and admirers from around the world. One of the many who spoke that night was Mary McLeod Bethune, the founder of the National Council of Negro Women and of what is now Bethune-Cookman College. In her remarks, Mrs. Bethune described Mr. Robeson as "the tallest tree in our forest."

Indeed, Paul Robeson brought to mind a most glorious tree. A towering presence on the earth. One grand and beautiful.

He was an extraordinary human being. Athlete. Scholar.

Singer. Lawyer. Shakespearean actor. Movie star. Author. Courageous fighter against bigotry and injustice. Hero.

All this in one lifetime. Seventy-seven years.

Paul Robeson was the son of a man who escaped from slavery at the age of fifteen. He was a brother to four other children in the Robeson family. He became a husband, and a father to one son.

His magnificent talents were praised all over the world. Among the best known of them was his beautiful baritone voice. Deep and rich, it flowed like a sweet, clear stream whose bottom had no end. He used that voice to express his love for beauty, such as when he sang the "Sorrow Songs." Spirituals. Songs created by black people who had been enslaved in America. That same brilliant voice supported the fights of people across the world—including his own black people in America—struggling to gain their equal rights.

His words, like his voice, were powerful. He said many

things he strongly felt needed to be said. Brave words of protest that spoke of wrongs needing to be made right, injustices deserving to be made fair. Often in his protests Paul Robeson expressed ideas that some did not want to hear. Especially those who had their own ideas about what it means to be a loyal American and what such Americans should not express out loud. Some of these people had powerful positions and the ways to silence—if only for a while—this great voice.

Paul Robeson was labeled "un-American." Theaters, concert halls, and recording studios across America felt that they would take on trouble if they hired him to perform. His passport was taken away, making it impossible for him to travel out of the United States. Thus, because of his beliefs and his determination to share them in order to empower others, Paul Robeson was denied the right to earn a living.

After ten years passed, Mr. Robeson was given back his passport and the right to bring his talents again to the world. But the years had taken their toll. Because of sickness, he never became again in life what he had been and what his tremendous talents still promised.

Paul Robeson passed from this life in 1976. Thousands of people attended his funeral and heard recordings of the spirituals his magnificent voice had celebrated throughout his career.

Messages expressing the sorrow of his passing came from around the world. One from a black man who had been imprisoned stood out from many of the rest.

They knocked the leaves from his limbs,
The bark from his tree;
But his roots were so deep
That they are a part of me.

Paul Robeson has been described as one of the greatest lives of the twentieth century. A giant of a man. Find out for yourself why this is so. There are many ways to do this; a few are listed here.

In looking for information, remember the value of having a conversation with someone in your home or community who knew about him. You might even come across someone who knew someone who actually met him. Or heard him sing. Or shook one of those magnificent hands.

While gathering information for this book, I came across such a person. Her name is Susan Woodson and she owns a gallery in Chicago filled with beautiful art.

She met Paul Robeson when she was a young girl, traveling to Chicago for the first time. I had many, many questions to ask her about Mr. Robeson. "Was his speaking voice deep and booming, like his singing voice? He was such a brilliant man—was it hard to talk with him? What were his eyes like when he looked at you?"

Mrs. Woodson told me that the only thing she could remember, truthfully, were his hands. "Huge. They were simply huge!" Then she reminded me that when she met Paul Robeson, she was a teenager with little interest in *any* adult, even a famous man with huge hands.

Whatever she remembered or didn't, I'm delighted to have met her and to know beyond all doubt that one of the men who has often been portrayed as greater than life was quite real.

BOOKS

• *Here I Stand*, written by Paul Robeson, first published in 1958.

Written in Paul Robeson's own words, this book opens an important door of understanding about what he believed in most and hoped to accomplish with his life and talents.

• *The Young Paul Robeson: "On My Journey Now,"* written by Lloyd Brown, published in 1997 by Westview Press.

The author of this book was one of Paul Robeson's close friends. The two worked together on some of Mr. Robeson's writings.

• *The Whole World in His Hands: A Pictorial Biography of Paul Robeson*, written by Susan Robeson, published in 1999 by Citadel Press.

This book, developed by Paul Robeson's granddaughter, provides a collection of photographs of Mr. Robeson, showing him during all stages of his life and careers.

• *Paul Robeson: The Life and Times of a Free Black Man*, written by Virginia Hamilton, published in 1974 by Harper & Row.

This biography of Paul Robeson was written by one of America's award-winning authors of books for children.

• *Paul Robeson: A Biography*, written by Martin Duberman, published by Alfred A. Knopf, 1988.
This book is a detailed and comprehensive examination of Paul Robeson's life. The information provided in the book was gathered from historical records and documents as well as from interviews with people who knew Mr. Robeson.

• *The Undiscovered Paul Robeson*, written by Paul Robeson, Jr., published in 2001 by John Wiley & Sons, Inc.
The author of this book is Paul Robeson's son.

FILMS

Note to Readers: In the times during which Paul Robeson was asked to act in movies, those who had the power and money to make films often had limited ideas and information about black people. Their visions about the kinds of roles blacks should play were also greatly limited. In some instances, Mr. Robeson believed that he would be able to present a better image or use his acting to tell a greater truth. Sadly, in many of these instances it did not turn out as he had thought. Because of this, he eventually became the first black person in the history of film to have the right of final approval of his films. In any instance, it is strongly suggested that his films be viewed with an understanding of the times in which they were made.

Some of the films can be found (in videotape formats) in public libraries. Some are available on VHS cassettes or DVDs and can be found in DVD/video-rental establishments.
• *Body and Soul* (1924). This was Mr. Robeson's first film and one made by the black filmmaker Oscar Micheaux.
• *The Emperor Jones* (1933)
• *Song of Freedom* (1936)
• *Big Fella* (1937)
• *Jericho* (1937)
• *Sanders of the River* (1937)
• *The Proud Valley* (1940)
• *Tales of Manhattan* (1942)

Several film productions exist that offer biographical information about Mr. Robeson and his times; two such titles follow. The first provides a broad sketch of his life. The second includes a segment telling about Mr. Robeson's fight for human rights and the consequences he suffered because of this commitment.

- *Scandalize My Name: Stories from the Blacklist* (1998)
- *Paul Robeson: Here I Stand* (1999)

RECORDINGS

- *Paul Robeson: The Legendary Moscow Concert*, recorded live in Moscow on June 14, 1949; available on audiocassette and CD
- *Great Voices of the Century: Paul Robeson*, a compilation of excerpts from Paul Robeson's performances; available on audiocassette and CD

INTERNET

Use your favorite search engine (for example, Google) and choose a keyword such as Robeson to search the Web for information about Paul Robeson. Addresses of two sites are listed below.

http://prcc.rutgers.edu/Robeson/biography.htm
http://www.pbs.org/wnet/americanmasters/
database/robeson_p.html

A FOREST OF TALENT

If you would like to find out about some of the other "tall trees" mentioned in this book, the following information can help you begin your search.

Marian Anderson, internationally famous classical musician; first African American to perform at the New York Metropolitan Opera
http://www.mariananderson.org/

Josephine Baker, internationally famous entertainer; activist
http://www.cmgworldwide.com/stars/baker/

Harry Belafonte, internationally honored entertainer and widely respected activist
http://www.belafonte-asiteofsites.com

Mary McLeod Bethune, educator; activist; founder of Bethune-Cookman College
http://www.nahc.org/NAHC/Val/Columns/SC10-6.html

Cabell "Cab" Calloway, internationally famous showman and bandleader
http://www.npr.org/programs/jazzprofiles/archive/calloway.html

Countee Cullen, poet, playwright, scholar
http://www.english.uiuc.edu/maps/poets/a_f/cullen/cullen.htm

Katherine Dunham, dancer, choreographer, and anthropologist
http://lcweb2.loc.gov/diglib/ihas/html/dunham/dunham-lifedance.html

Edward Kennedy "Duke" Ellington, internationally famous composer, musician, and bandleader
http://www.pbs.org/jazz/biography/artist_id_ellington_duke.htm

Roland Hayes, first internationally applauded African-American male concert musician
http://www.bridgew.edu/HOBA/Hayes.cfm

Lena Horne, star of stage and screen; civil rights activist
http://www.pbs.org/newshour/bb/entertainment/
june97/horne_6-30.html

Oscar Micheaux, pioneer filmmaker
http://shorock.com/arts/micheaux/

Bill Pickett, cowboy and legendary rodeo performer
http://www.famoustexans.com/billpickett.htm

William Warfield, internationally recognized singer, music educator
http://www.riverwalkjazz.org/site/PageServer?pagename=
profiles_warfield

Booker T. Washington, educator and activist; founder of Tuskegee Institute
http://www.nps.gov/archive/bowa/btwbio.html

Ethel Waters, often referred to as the first African-American superstar
http://www.redhotjazz.com/waters.html

Carter G. Woodson, scholar, educator, and founder of Negro History Week (which is celebrated today as Black History Month)
http://www.chipublib.org/002branches/woodson/woodsonbib. html

Susan Cayton Woodson, art gallery founder and owner; great-granddaughter of Hiram R. Revels, the first African-American senator
http://www.thehistorymakers.com/biography/biography.asp ?bioindex=642

The author and publisher wish to thank the following for permission to reproduce the photographs of Paul Robeson in this book.

Special Collections and University Archives, Rutgers University Libraries: Pages 8, 30, 50, 82, 104, 122, *From the* Scarlet Letter *yearbook, 1919.* Page 18, *In a football uniform, ca. 1916–1918.* Page 42, *Member of the Cap and Skull Society, from the* Scarlet Letter *yearbook, ca. 1919.*

The Paul Robeson Foundation, Inc., courtesy of Paul Robeson, Jr.: Page 64, Othello, *Savoy Theatre, London, 1930.* Page 96, *Moscow Concert, with accompanist Larry Brown, 1936.* Page 112, *world premiere at London's largest theatre, 1936.* Page 136, *Concert for Naval Workers, 1942.*

Poem on page 143 enclosed in a letter to Judge George W. Crockett, November 6, 1977, from Bill [*sic*] Brown. Reprinted courtesy of Paul Robeson, Jr.